Suddenly, strange little Hob-the-
Goblin popped up and snatched
Raggedy Andy's cap right off
his cotton-stuffed head!
"Finders keepers!" cried Hob.
"Catch me if you can!" And off
he ran wearing Andy's best and
only blue and white cap.
"Come on, Raggedy Ann," said Andy,
"let's get him."

The Raggedys chased the goblin, and they chased him right into a hole in the ground. Down, down they tumbled until they hit the bottom, which didn't hurt their cotton-stuffed bodies a bit. And what do you think? They found themselves in a great ice cavern all hung about with gleaming colored icicles! They looked around, but there was no sign of Hob-the-Goblin.

"Let's think what to do," said Raggedy Ann.

"You'll have to think for both of us," said Andy. "I can't think worth a nickel without my hat on." He broke off a piece of icicle and sucked it. "Lemon soda-water!" he cried.

"I wonder if that one is my favorite flavor... root beer?" Raggedy Ann exclaimed.

Well, is it root beer? Let's see for ourselves. Scratch and sniff.

The Raggedys were munching on icicles when they saw Hob-the-Goblin racing toward them on ice skates.

"Hand over my hat or I'll wrestle you good!" shouted Andy.

"Come and get it!" cried Hob-the-Goblin. But when Raggedy Ann and Andy tried to stand up they found that they were frozen to the ice floor! "Haha!" Hob-the-Goblin crowed, "The icicles have melted and run through your cotton stuffing and now you are stuck! And that's the way you're going to stay!" he howled, and skated away.

"I'm not going home without my cap, Raggedy Ann. It's part of me, just like your candy heart is part of you," said Andy.

"I know, Andy," said Raggedy Ann, "but we can't get your cap unless we get unstuck." And she opened her mouth as wide as she could and yelled "HELP!"

Andy didn't think that anyone would hear, but someone did!
A little real-for-sure cookie person ran out from behind an ice
pillar. "Are you lost?" she asked sweetly and then announced,
"I am! I've been lost ever since I was a cookie baby and a
beautiful golden butterfly flew by my cookie crib, and I followed it
and never got home again. Now tell me, how did you get lost?"

"We're not so much lost as stuck," explained Raggedy Ann,
and she told the little lost cookie about their adventures.

"That's the saddest thing I've ever heard," said Little Lost Cookie. "I finally meet two nice friends to play with and they're stuck to the floor!" Little Lost Cookie gulped, snuffled, and began to cry. She cried so hard that her warm tears melted the ice all around the Raggedys.

"We're free!" exclaimed Raggedy Ann.

"Look," said Andy. "Hob-the-Goblin has left a trail with his ice skates...let's follow it!"

So they followed the trail right to a big door. They opened the door, and went inside.

"A bakery!" Raggedy Ann cried. "Doesn't it smell delicious?"

"This must be Cookie-Land!" cried Little Lost Cookie, delightedly.

Suddenly Hob-the-Goblin jumped out of a giant cookie jar. "These goodies are mine! All mine! And you can't have any!" he yelled, stuffing a fistful of cookies into his mouth.

*Do you like
cinnamon cookies?
What a delicious smell.
Scratch and sniff.*

"Who's been gobbling at my cookies?" a great voice boomed, and the strangest big man came stomping toward them. He picked up Hob-the-Goblin and shook him. "You're a cookie eater, and that's against the law!" the man growled. "I'm going to put you through the great roller and then you'll be sorry." The strange man pushed a button and the great roller began to move!

"Help, help, help!" shrieked Hob-the-Goblin, and he gave the strange man a push. SNAP! the man broke right in two!

"Why, he's nothing but a cookie man," exclaimed Hob. "He's made of yummy chocolate dough! I shall eat him!"

"Oh, no you won't," said Andy fiercely, holding on to Hob with all his might. Then Andy and Little Cookie threw Hob out the big door and slammed it shut behind him.

Scratch and sniff the sticky licorice taffy.

"Thank goodness he's gone!" said Raggedy Ann. "Now, however can we fix this poor broken cookie man?"

"I know!" said Little Lost Cookie, running over to a pot of licorice taffy. Then they pasted the cookie man back together again and even made him a brand new icing suit.

"Thank you, thank you!" said Mr. Cookie, jumping up. "Mrs. Cookie will be so grateful. You must come home with me and meet her."

Mrs. Cookie was waiting for them outside a cunning little cookie cottage. When she heard the story of Mr. Cookie's rescue she was so grateful that she ran to the cupboard and brought out three large cookies with the word *"bravery"* written on them. "I've been saving these medals for just such an occasion," she said as she pinned them on Raggedy Ann, Andy, and Little Lost Cookie. Then she announced, "We are having roast cake chicken with cherry pecan stuffing for supper. Please stay."

"Oh! May we help stuff the chicken?" asked Little Lost Cookie, who was feeling very much at home.

"Of course you may," Mrs. Cookie replied. "Andy, would you go out to the garden and pick some desserts? The pie bushes are in bloom and I believe the mince pies are deliciously ripe!"

Raggedy Andy was picking a fragrant mince pie when he saw Hob-the-Goblin, and with him was a Snitznoodle!

"This Snitznoodle here is going to tie you up in knots so I can get inside and gobble up the cookie people!" the Goblin said.

But the Snitznoodle had spied the bravery medal on Andy's jacket. "Oh, no. I won't fight him!" the Snitznoodle cried. "Anyone with a bravery medal would be too hard to wrestle."

Have you ever sniffed a ripe mince pie?

"Fiddlesticks!" yelled Hob. "After him!" And he thumped the Snitznoodle hard on the head.

The Snitznoodle didn't like that one bit. "Have *you* got a bravery medal, Hob?" he inquired.

"No, I haven't, you silly!" screeched the Goblin.

"Then take *that*!" said the Snitznoodle and he thumped Hob back. "Never ask me to help you again," he said, as he and Raggedy Andy walked back to the cookie house arm in arm.

"This is my new friend, the brave Snitznoodle," Andy said.

"I hope you'll stay for supper," Mrs. Cookie suggested.

"Thank you, but I couldn't eat a thing!" the Snitznoodle replied.
"I had a dozen wind sandwiches on my way here!"

"Wind sandwiches! May I try one?" asked Little Lost Cookie.

"Alrighty," said the Snitznoodle. "First cut two thin slices of air.
Then spread a lump of soft wind on each slice, place them together so...
and there you have it, a mighty tasty wind sandwich!"

Everyone took a bite but no one found it very tasty. "Try this, Mr. Snitznoodle!" said Mrs. Cookie as she presented him with a steaming bowl of chocolate soup. The Snitznoodle slurped a spoonful, just to be polite.

"My, but this soup is scrumptious!" he exclaimed. "Even better than wind sandwiches!"

Scratch and sniff to smell Mrs. Cookie's scrumptious chocolate soup.

The Snitznoodle immediately offered to protect the Cookie family from Hob-the-Goblin twenty-four hours a day with time out for breakfast, lunch, tea, dinner, and midnight snacks of chocolate soup.

"We'd love to have you," laughed Mr. Cookie.

"I'll just run home and get my nightie!" the Snitznoodle said.

"Don't start dinner without me!" He dashed out the door.

"I hope he doesn't take too long," said Raggedy Andy. "I'm hungry."

"You can help me set the table while we're waiting," said Little Lost Cookie, beginning to scurry around. "Oops!" she exclaimed, as she dropped a fork and bent over to pick it up.

"Oh, my, oh, my!" Mrs. Cookie suddenly cried. "Why, Little Lost Cookie, you have a raisin behind your knee just like... oh, could it be?... come look, Mr. Cookie... our long lost daughter, Little Raisin!"

Little Raisin ran into their outstretched arms, crying, "Mother, Father!"

The Raggedys celebrated Little Raisin's homecoming by playing and singing a favorite old song, "Love's Return."

Suddenly there was a loud banging at the front door. "It's your friendly neighborhood Snitznoodle," growled a gruff voice.

"Oh, no it's not," said Raggedy Ann. "I know your voice, Hob-the-Goblin. You'd better run before the Snitznoodle comes back!"

"Open the door," Hob howled. "I've come to live with the nice yummy cookie people!"

"Mercy, no! He'd eat us up!" cried Mrs. Cookie.

"I *am* hungry," said Hob, "and if you don't open the door then I'll nibble my way in."

You wouldn't eat the nice Cookie family's peppermint door, or would you? Scratch and sniff.

And just as he said, the Goblin nibbled a large hole in the front door and put his head through it. But Andy and Mr. Cookie quickly grabbed him by his pointy ears and held him fast while Raggedy Ann climbed out a window with a large pancake paddle.

My, how Hob-the-Goblin howled when Raggedy Ann

paddywhacked him with the paddle! "Enough!" cried the Goblin, twisting and kicking. "I give up—I'll be a good Goblin from now on!"

Raggedy Andy and Mr. Cookie let go of Hob's ears and he pulled his head out of the cookie door.

"Thank you, thank you," Hob sniffled. "I've learned that being mean isn't any fun. I don't have a friend in the world."

"There, there," said Raggedy Ann, dabbing at his tears with her pocket hankie. "It's never too late to make friends."

"Here's your cap, Raggedy Andy," said Hob as he took it out of his back pocket. "You know, I've eaten so much door cake that I feel all sweet and sentimental inside."

Everyone sat down to a magnificent dinner. They had seconds, thirds, and fourths of cake chicken and mince pies.

Raggedy Ann stood and said, "I'd like to propose a toast," and she raised high her glass of sparkling cherry soda. "To my dear friends... thank you one and all for this wonderful feast."

"And for a terrific adventure!" added Raggedy Andy.

"And now I'm afraid it's time for Andy and me to return home to our nursery," said Raggedy Ann solemnly.